To Laurent Linn,
who always encourages me
to color outside the lines

SIMON & SCHUSTER BOOKS FOR YOUNG READERS
An imprint of Simon & Schuster Children's Publishing Division
1230 Avenue of the Americas, New York, New York 10020
Copyright © 2017 by Debbie Ridpath Ohi
All rights reserved, including the right of reproduction in whole or in part in any form.
SIMON & SCHUSTER BOOKS FOR YOUNG READERS is a trademark of Simon & Schuster, Inc.
For information about special discounts for bulk purchases,
please contact Simon & Schuster Special Sales at 1-866-506-1949 or business@simonandschuster.com.
The Simon & Schuster Speakers Bureau can bring authors to your live event. For more information or to book an event,
contact the Simon & Schuster Speakers Bureau at 1-866-248-3049 or visit our website at www.simonspeakers.com.
Book design by Laurent Linn
The text for this book was set in Plumbsky.
The illustrations for this book were rendered digitally.
Manufactured in China
0717 SCP
First Edition
2 4 6 8 10 9 7 5 3 1
Library of Congress Cataloging-in-Publication Data
Names: Ohi, Debbie Ridpath, 1962- author, illustrator.
Title: Sam & Eva / Debbie Ridpath Ohi.
Other titles: Sam and Eva
Description: First edition. | New York : Simon & Schuster Books for Young Readers, [2017] | Summary: Sam does not want Eva to add to his drawing,
but when the scene comes to life and gets out of control, she helps him escape. Identifiers: LCCN 2016036135 (print) | LCCN 2017014063 (ebook)
ISBN 9781481416283 (hardcover) | ISBN 9781481416290 (Ebook)
Subjects: | CYAC: Drawing—Fiction. | Cooperativeness—Fiction.
Classification: LCC PZ7.O414034 (ebook) | LCC PZ7.O414034 Sam 2017 (print) | DDC [E]—dc23
LC record available at https://lccn.loc.gov/2016036135

SAM & EVA

Debbie Ridpath Ohi

SIMON & SCHUSTER BOOKS FOR YOUNG READERS

NEW YORK   LONDON   TORONTO   SYDNEY   NEW DELHI

Sam had just begun to draw when Eva arrived.

"I like your pony," Eva said.

"It's a velociraptor," said Sam.

Eva suggested a collaboration.

Sam declined.

"Who said you could add a cat?"
asked Sam.

"It's not a cat," Eva said.
"It's a marmot."

Sam's velociraptor was hungry.

Luckily, Eva's marmot had a friend.

So did Sam's velociraptor.

Marmot was actually
a superhero in disguise.

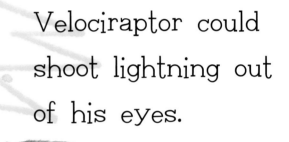

Velociraptor could
shoot lightning out
of his eyes.

Suddenly, a giant piano
fell from the sky and squashed
Marmot and her friend!

Suddenly, a giant piano confetti
fell from the sky and squashed tickled
Marmot and her friend!

Marmot liked the confetti UNTIL

"I don't like this story anymore," said Eva.

Sam kept drawing,
but it wasn't the same.

"I think it's time to start a new story," said Eva.

"Draw fast!" said Sam.

"I like your unicorn," said Sam.

"It's a triceratops," said Eva.